I Am a Tyrannosaurus

TATSUYA MIYANISHI

MUSEYON, New York

A long, long, really long time ago,
there were a mom and dad Pteranodon.

Mom laid an egg on the top of
a rocky mountain.

One night
the egg rolled around and . . .

Mom and Dad Pteranodon
were filled with joy.
The couple raised the baby
with great care.

Dad Pteranodon gave the baby lots of food.

He said, "Eat well, my son, and grow strong."

Mom Pteranodon rocked the baby to sleep.
She said, "Grow up to be kind."

Dad showed him how to
fly in the sky.

"Open your wings as
wide as you can,
and push against the
ground with all your
strength.

Then catch the wind.
When you fly high, you
won't even have to worry
about the nasty, scary
Tyrannosaurus."

Mom covered the baby
with her wings on cold,
rainy days so that he
wouldn't get wet.
"You must help anyone
who is in trouble,"
she said.

The baby Pteranodon grew quickly and was soon almost as big as his dad.

One night Dad Pteranodon looked at their sleeping son and said to Mom, "Our baby has grown big. It's time to say good-bye."

"Do you think he will be all right by himself?"
"He'll be fine. He is almost a full-grown Pteranodon."

But . . . can he fly well enough?"
"He's old enough to take care of himself," Dad said.
Mom shed a tear.

Then the two Pteranodons flew away.
It was a very quiet night indeed.

Morning arrived.

The young Pteranodon woke up.
Oh! Mom and Dad aren't here.
I wonder where they have gone.
Maybe they went looking for food?

He waited a long, long time, but
Mom and Dad did not come back.
"Daaad! Mooommm!"
The young Pteranodon
called many, many times.

Then he got tired of calling and fell asleep. Just then, from below . . .

Just as he was
about to grab
the young
Pteranodon . . .

Booom!

A nearby volcano erupted!
The earth
shook, shook, shook. . . .
The Tyrannosaurus tumbled
down, down, down. . . .

CRAAAASH!

The Tyrannosaurus slammed into the ground.
When the young Pteranodon went down to see what
had happened, the Tyrannosaurus was moaning in pain.
"Oooohhh . . ."

The young Pteranodon wondered what to do
because he remembered that his dad had said
the Tyrannosaurus was a nasty, scary creature.

After a while, the Tyrannosaurus stopped moving.
Then the young Pteranodon remembered what his mom had said:
"You must help anyone who is in trouble."

All right, he thought.
The young Pteranodon carried the rocks away, one by one.

After a while all the rocks were gone, but the
Tyrannosaurus still did not move.
Is he all right? the young Pteranodon wondered.

"Ooh, ouch! I . . . I can't move my body. I can't see anything.
What's happening?" The Tyrannosaurus groaned.
He was badly injured.

Shocked by the sound of the voice, the young Pteranodon said
without thinking, "I . . . I'm—no, I mean—I'm a Tyrannosaurus. . . ."

"A Tyrannosaurus like me?
Then why is your voice so cute and small?"

"Tha . . . that's because if I spoke loudly, it might hurt you.
Understand!?" The young Pteranodon used
all his strength and shouted
as loudly as he could.

The young Pteranodon felt sorry for the wounded Tyrannosaurus and decided to look after him.

When it rained, the young Pteranodon
covered the Tyrannosaurus with leaves
so that his body would not get wet.

He took care of the Tyrannosaurus with
gentleness and kindness, just as
his mom had done for him.

The young Pteranodon fed the Tyrannosaurus red berries.

"Do they taste good?"
"Yeah . . . they taste good."
"Actually, fish would tastes better,
but I still can't fly to the ocean. . . .
Oh, I mean jump to the ocean."
The Tyrannosaurus heard what the young Pteranodon
said but did not reply.

The young Pteranodon gathered red berries and
fed the Tyrannosaurus plenty and plenty more, just
as his dad had done for him.

Many, many days passed.
Then one night the young Pteranodon came back carrying
red berries, and saw the Tyrannosaurus with his blazing eyes
open and a fish in his mouth.

He . . . he's standing! He can see too!
The surprised young Pteranodon dropped the red berries.

Hearing the sound of the falling berries . . .

the Tyrannosaurus turned around.
Then, with the fish in his mouth,
he charged toward the young Pteranodon.

Wh . . . what should I do?
The young Pteranodon remembered what his
dad had said:

"Open your wings as wide as you can,
and push against the ground with all your strength.
Then catch the wind. When you fly high, you won't even
have to worry about the nasty, scary Tyrannosaurus."

The young Pteranodon opened his wings as wide as he could.
"Here I go!"

Then catch the wind.

The young Pteranodon felt the wind on his wings. "It's just as Dad told me. I'm flying!"

Riding on the southern wind, the young Pteranodon soared into the sky.

From high up in the sky, the young Pteranodon looked down at the Tyrannosaurus, who looked very small, and thought,

I'm glad that the Tyrannosaurus got better. I'm happy that he can see again. If I were a real Tyrannosaurus, maybe we could have been good friends. . . . Good-bye, Tyrannosaurus!

The Tyrannosaurus stopped chasing the young Pteranodon. He looked up into the starry sky and mumbled,

I knew all along that you were a Pteranodon. I got the fish that you love to eat so I could share it with you. I wanted to look into your eyes and say, "Thank you."

The Tyrannosaurus stared at the sky into which the young Pteranodon had disappeared.

"Thank you," he said.

"THANK YOU!"

About Author

Born in 1956, **Tatsuya Miyanishi** is one of the most popular children's book creators in Japan. His Tyrannosaurus series has sold more than three million copies and has been translated into many languages. Miyanishi has won the Kodansha Cultural Award for Picture Books, as well as the Kenbuchi Picture Book Grand Prize.

I AM A TYRANNOSAURUS

Ore wa Tyrannosaurus da © 2004 Tatsuya Miyanishi
All rights reserved.

Publisher's Cataloging-in-Publication Data
Names: Miyanishi, Tatsuya, 1956- author, illustrator. | Gharbi, Marido Shii, translator. | Kaplan, Simone, editor.
Title: I am a tyrannosaurus / Tatsuya Miyanishi ; translation by Mariko Shii Gharbi ; English editing by Simone Kaplan.
Other titles: Ore wa tyrannosaurus. English
Description: New York : Museyon, [2018] | Series: Tyrannosaurus series ; book 5. | "Originally published in Japan in 2004 by POPLAR Publishing Co., Ltd."--Title page verso. |
Identifiers: ISBN: 9781940842240 | LCCN: 2017919165
Subjects: LCSH: Tyrannosaurus rex- Juvenile fiction. | Pterosauria- Juvenile fiction. | Dinosaurs-Juvenile fiction. | Kindness- Juvenile fiction. | Helping behavior in children- Juvenile fiction. | CYAC: Tyrannosaurus rex- Fiction. | Pterosaurs- Fiction. | Dinsosaurs- Fiction. | Kindness- Fiction. | Helpfullness- Fiction. | LCGFT: Picture books. | BISAC: JUVENILE FICTION / Animals / Dinosaurs & Prehistoric Creatures.
Classification: LCC: PZ7.M699575 O7413 2018 | DDC: [E]--dc23

Published in the United States and Canada by:
Museyon Inc.
333 East 45th Street
New York, NY 10017

Museyon is a registered trademark.
Visit us online at www.museyon.com

Originally published in Japan in 2004 by POPLAR Publishing Co., Ltd.
English translation rights arranged with POPLAR Publishing Co., Ltd.

Printed in China

ISBN 9781940842240